I0591559

Off Off Broadway Festival Plays, 39th Series

et•y•mol•o•gy
by Jennifer Jasper

John, Who's Here From Cambridge
by Martyna Majok

The Logic
by Will Arbery

Mandate
by Kelly Younger

Taisetsu Na Hito
by Leah Nanako Winkler

A Wake for David's Fucked-Up Face
by Skylar Fox

A SAMUEL FRENCH ACTING EDITION

SAMUEL FRENCH

FOUNDED 1830

SAMUELFRENCH.COM
SAMUELFRENCH-LONDON.CO.UK

FOR PRODUCTION ENQUIRIES

UNITED STATES AND CANADA
Info@SamuelFrench.com
1-866-598-8449

UNITED KINGDOM AND EUROPE
Plays@SamuelFrench-London.co.uk
020-7255-4302

Each title is subject to availability from Samuel French, depending upon country of performance. Please be aware that *ET•Y•MOL•O•GY, JOHN, WHO'S HERE FROM CAMBRIDGE, THE LOGIC, MANDATE, TAISETSU NA HITO,* and/or *A WAKE FOR DAVID'S FUCKED-UP FACE* may not be licensed by Samuel French in your territory. Professional and amateur producers should contact the nearest Samuel French office or licensing partner to verify availability.

CAUTION: Professional and amateur producers are hereby warned that *ET•Y•MOL•O•GY, JOHN, WHO'S HERE FROM CAMBRIDGE, THE LOGIC, MANDATE, TAISETSU NA HITO,* and/or *A WAKE FOR DAVID'S FUCKED-UP FACE* is subject to a licensing fee. Publication of this play(s) does not imply availability for performance. Both amateurs and professionals considering a production are strongly advised to apply to Samuel French before starting rehearsals, advertising, or booking a theatre. A licensing fee must be paid whether the title(s) is presented for charity or gain and whether or not admission is charged. Professional/Stock licensing fees are quoted upon application to Samuel French.

No one shall make any changes in this title(s) for the purpose of production. No part of this book may be reproduced, stored in a retrieval system, or transmitted in any form, by any means, now known or yet to be invented, including mechanical, electronic, photocopying, recording, videotaping, or otherwise, without the prior written permission of the publisher. No one shall upload this title(s), or part of this title(s), to any social media websites.

For all enquiries regarding motion picture, television, and other media rights, please contact Samuel French.

MUSIC USE NOTE

Licensees are solely responsible for obtaining formal written permission from copyright owners to use copyrighted music in the performance of this play and are strongly cautioned to do so. If no such permission is obtained by the licensee, then the licensee must use only original music that the licensee owns and controls. Licensees are solely responsible and liable for all music clearances and shall indemnify the copyright owners of the play(s) and their licensing agent, Samuel French, against any costs, expenses, losses and liabilities arising from the use of music by licensees. Please contact the appropriate music licensing authority in your territory for the rights to any incidental music.

IMPORTANT BILLING AND CREDIT REQUIREMENTS

If you have obtained performance rights to this title, please refer to your licensing agreement for important billing and credit requirements.

The Samuel French Off Off Broadway Short Play Festival started in 1975 and is one of the nation's most established and highly regarded short play festivals. During the course of the Festival's 39 years, over 500 theatre companies and schools participated in the Festival, including companies from coast to coast as well as abroad from Canada, Singapore, and the United Kingdom. Over the years, more than 200 submitted plays have been published, with many of the participants becoming established, award-winning playwrights.

Festival Co-Artistic Directors: Amy Rose Marsh and Casey McLain
Associate Literary Coordinator: Ben Coleman
Judge Coordinator: Abbie Van Nostrand
Marketing Director: Ryan Pointer
Marketing Coordinators: Chris Kam and Courtney Kochuba
Stage Manager: Laura Manos-Hey
House Manager: Tyler Mullen
Executive Director: Bruce Lazarus
Festival Interns: Alex Davis and Meyers Rhoad
Festival Staff: Caitlin Bartow, Charlyn Brea, Ashley Byrne,
Coryn Carson, Nick Dawson, BJ Evans, Joe Ferreira, Dyan Flores,
David Geer, Glenn Halcomb, Laura Lindson, Elizabeth Minski,
Kim Rogers, Charlie Sou, Annette Storckman, and Sarah Weber

FESTIVAL KEYNOTE SPEAKER
Doug Wright

GUEST JUDGES
Keith Josef Adkins
Leslie Ayvazian
Neena Beber
Rick Burkhardt
Adam Greenfield
Alex Kilgore
Dave Malloy
Emily Morse
Christian Parker
Maria Striar
Mac Wellman
Susan Westfall

For more information on the Samuel French Off Off Broadway Short
Play Festival, including history, interviews, and more, please visit
www.oob.samuelfrench.com.

FESTIVAL PARTICIPANTS
- THE TOP 30 -

ATTILA by Ben Samuels
THE BASKET WEAVER by Blaire Baron Larsen
BENCH by Ann Gillespie
BUDDY HOLLY AT THE ARMORY by Zac Kline
DEBRIDEMENT by Megan Dieterle
ENDNOTE by Meridith Friedman
ET•Y•MOL•O•GY by Jennifer Jasper
EVERYBODY HURTS (SOMETIMES) by Emily Dendinger
FURBALL by Susan Soon He Stanton
THE IDYLLIC LIFE: A BAVARIAN FAIRY TALE by Jay Koepke
IT LOOKED LIKE RAIN by Donna Noval
***JOHN, WHO'S HERE FROM CAMBRIDGE* by Martyna Majok**
LAVINIA by Jon Lachlan Stewart
LIFE OF THE PARTY by Matthew Widman
THE *LOGIC* by Will Arbery
***MANDATE* by Kelly Younger**
THE MATTHEW PORTRAITS by Collette Mazunik
NO STRANGER THERE by Luke Wise
OH, HOW HE LOVED BAKLAVA by Trish Harnetiaux
OUTSIDE SITKA by Josh Billig
PARK SLOPE MINSTREL SHOW by Eleanor Burgess
PROM QUEEN by David Simpatico
RED AND PURPLE by Conor Eifler
RUBY'S PLAY by Ariel Rosen-Brown
SHREW MAN VS. SHREWMAN by C.J. Ehrlich
SPLAT GOES YOUR DAY by Sarah Einspanier
***TAISETSU NA HITO* by Leah Nanako Winkler**
UNKEMPT by Rebecca Schlossberg
***A WAKE FOR DAVID'S FUCKED-UP FACE* by Skylar Fox**
XANDER XYST, DRAGON: PART 1 by Jeremy O. Harris

CONTENTS

et·y·mol·o·gy

Jennifer Jasper

ET•Y•MOL•O•GY was first produced as part of 14/48: The World's Quickest Theater Festival in Seattle, Washington in January 2013. The performance was directed by John Langs. The cast was as follows:

SUSAN ANNE . . . . Emma Bamford
CALVIN . . . . .Darius Pierce

ET•Y•MOL•O•GY was produced by the 14/48 Projects and Kathie Whitehall as part of the Samuel French Off Off Broadway Short Play Festival at the Peter J. Sharp Theatre, Playwrights Horizons in New York City on August 8, 2014. The performance was directed by Shawn Belyea. The cast was as follows:

SUSAN ANNE . . . . Megan Ahiers
CALVIN . . . . .Trick Danneker

CHARACTERS

CALVIN

SUSAN ANNE

SETTING

A spelling bee – and other places

LIGHTING

Shifts can be used for transitions, but are not necessary.

SOUND

A bell sound signifies correct spelling.

SET

Two chairs – which can be used in various ways (desks, couch, etc)

ABOUT THE PLAYWRIGHT

Jennifer Jasper is a storyteller, performer, playwright and director who has been a part of the Seattle theater community for more than two decades. She's known for her consummate storytelling, pristine timing and intuitive director's eye. As a performer and writer she possesses an uncanny capacity for creating memorable characters that are colorful, often outlandish and always emotionally authentic.

She has written and performed three autobiographical solo shows since 2012. Her first, *I Can Hear You…But I'm Not Listening* has been performed nationally. *It Will Kill Them!* premiered in 2014, and in 2015 her latest show *Bullygirl* met with critical success.

In 2016, a showcase of her work entitled *Pressing Matters*, produced by MBL Productions, Inc., will premiere Off Broadway in New York City.

Ms. Jasper was awarded one of eight Jack Straw Productions Artist Support grants in 2013 to record the stories from *I Can Hear You…But I'm Not Listening.* The stories from her solo work are due to be published in book form in 2015 by Dizzybess Press. She is a 2015 recipient of the Willapa Bay AiR.

She produces, hosts and curates a monthly cabaret entitled Family Affair– Cabaret served up family style at The JewelBox Theater in Seattle. All the acts center around the theme of family and each month the show raises money for a member of the arts family who is going through a personal crisis.

Ms. Jasper received her BA in Directing from the University of New Mexico. She co-founded the improvisational company Kings' Elephant Theatre. After a decade of critical and commercial success with Kings' Elephant, Jennifer went on to co-found Vixen Productions (1995–2005). This all-woman company toured and performed nationally. She was resident director for Printer's Devil Theatre (2009–2014). She is a regular participant in The 14/48 Projects.

She lives in Seattle, Washington with her wife and co-producer, Kathie Whitehall, and their 19-year-old cat, Irma Louise, also known as "The Immortal One."

JenniferJasperPerforms.com

(Both actors standing downstage of chairs.)

SUSAN ANNE. FLATULENCE. F-L-A-T-U-L-E-N-C-E.

*(**CALVIN** giggles – **SUSAN** glares at him.)*

(Lighting shift.)

*(Both are standing in line in a cafeteria – **SUSAN** in front of **CALVIN**.)*

SUSAN ANNE. *(to herself)* No, please, no. *(visibly squeezing her buttocks together and shifting)*

CALVIN. *(makes face as he smells something awful)* Ewww.

*(**SUSAN ANNE** looks down and is completely embarrassed to the point of tears.)*

CALVIN. *(stares at her and then pointing in a completely different direction)* EWW, PATRICK BUELL JUST FARTED!

*(**SUSAN ANNE** turns to look at him and he smiles at her.)*

(Light shift.)

SUSAN ANNE. FLATULENCE!

(Bell sounds.)

CALVIN. INFATUATION. I–N–F–A–T–U–A–T–I–O-N.

(Light shift.)

(Sitting at desks – one in front of the other – in class.)

SUSAN ANNE. *(turning around)* I want to be a professional speller.

CALVIN. Is that a real job?

SUSAN ANNE. I'm sure it is. Isn't it?

CALVIN. I want to be a pilot. I think that would be really cool. I love heights. And lightning. I want to see it up close. All bright. Then maybe discover what the Devil's Triangle is *really* about, solve it, you know, the mystery.

SUSAN ANNE. I think that would be more of an explorer, wouldn't it?

CALVIN. I guess so. But an explorer who flies planes. A pilotplorer.

SUSAN ANNE. That's a cool word. I like all the p's. So, do you want to go to Sadie Hawkins?

CALVIN. Uh, sure.

SUSAN ANNE. Ok. Cool.

(Light shift.)

CALVIN. INFATUATION!

(Bell sounds.)

SUSAN ANNE. MATRIMONY. M-A-T-R-I-M-O-N-Y.

(Light shift.)

(Both sitting on chairs facing each other – SUSAN ANNE has her feet in CALVIN's lap – she's doing a crossword, he's drinking coffee. Very relaxed.)

14 letters: A basic science that deals with heat, temperature, and energy.

CALVIN. Is there any more coffee? (pause) Thermodynamics.

SUSAN ANNE. I'd love some, thanks. (shifts)

CALVIN. Did you just fart?

SUSAN ANNE. Thermodynamics! (laughs)

CALVIN. Will you marry me?

(Light shift.)

SUSAN ANNE. MATRIMONY!

(Bell sounds.)

CALVIN. MISCARRIAGE. M-I-S-C-A-R-R-I-A-G-E.

(Light shift.)

(Both sitting back to back.)

(Watching a lightning storm – flash of light.)

CALVIN. 1, 2, 3, 4, 5.

(Clap of thunder.)

SUSAN ANNE. A-L-E-X-A-N-D-E-R.

CALVIN. You should come watch the storm.

SUSAN ANNE. *(whispers)* Alexander Xavier.

CALVIN. I'll make you some tea. *(doesn't move)*

SUSAN ANNE. X-A-V-I-E-R.

(Flash of light.)

CALVIN. 1,2,3.

(Clap of thunder.)

SUSAN. E-L-I-Z-A-B-E-T-H.

CALVIN. Peppermint ok?

SUSAN ANNE. Elizabeth Gwyneth.

(Clap of thunder.)

(Light shift.)

CALVIN. MISCARRIAGE.

(Bell sounds.)

SUSAN ANNE. INFIDELITY! I-N-F-I-D-E-L-I-T-Y.

(Light shift.)

(Driving in a car.)

FUCK YOU!

CALVIN. It was…

SUSAN ANNE. What? It was what, Calvin? What the fuck was it?

CALVIN. It was just…damn it. I don't know. I still don't know.

SUSAN ANNE. Is or Was? That's my question, Calvin. IS or WAS?

CALVIN. Was.

SUSAN ANNE. It didn't look like a WAS tonight. It looked like an IS. She looked like she thinks it's an IS. Is it?

CALVIN. Fuck.

SUSAN ANNE. Well put, Calvin. F-U-C-K. Fuck. Asshole. Fucking asshole.

(Light shift.)

SUSAN ANNE. INFIDELITY!

(Bell sounds.)

CALVIN. RECONCILIATION. R-E-C-O-N-C-I-L-I-A-T-I-O-N.

(Light shift.)

(Standing on deck of cruise ship.)

SUSAN ANNE. It's beautiful.

CALVIN. Calm after the storm.

SUSAN ANNE. I heard there were a lot of seasick people last night, some pretty pale people at the buffet this morning. A lot of wasted steaks.

CALVIN. We're supposed to be nearing the Triangle this afternoon. Cool.

SUSAN ANNE. You haven't said "cool" in years. It was so nice of the kids to give us this trip to Bermuda.

CALVIN. They are probably hoping we'll disappear.

SUSAN ANNE. Is anyone around us?

CALVIN. Why?

SUSAN ANNE. Because I just farted.

(Both laugh.)

(Light shift.)

CALVIN. RECONCILIATION.

(Bell sounds.)

SUSAN ANNE. ALZHEIMERS. A-L- *(begins again)* A-L —

(She stops unable to remember the word and steps back.)

CALVIN. ALZHEIMERS. A-L-Z-H-E-I-M-E-R-S.

(Light shift.)

(**SUSAN ANNE** *sits down,* **CALVIN** *joins her. She looks at him without reccgnition and stares into the distance. He touches her hand.)*

(Light shift.)

(Both actors stand and step forward.)

ALZHEIMERS.

(Bell sounds.)

(Both turn and shake hands and exit the stage flirting.)

(Fade out.)

John, Who's Here From Cambridge

Martyna Majok

JOHN, WHO'S HERE FROM CAMBRIDGE was produced as part of the Samuel French Off Off Broadway Short Play Festival at the Peter J. Sharp Theatre, Playwrights Horizons in New York City on August 6, 2014. The performance was directed by Nick Leavens. The cast was as follows:

JESS . . . . .Layla Khoshnoudi
JOHN . . . . Gregg Mozgala

JOHN, WHO'S HERE FROM CAMBRIDGE was originally produced as part of EST/Youngblood's TAKE THIS JOB AND BRUNCH IT Festival of Short Plays, held in New York City on March 2, 2014 with the same director and cast.

CHARACTERS

JESS – a woman in her late 20s/early 30s; does not come from wealth; a part-time cocktail waitress.

JOHN – a man in his late 20s/early 30s; comes from wealth; has cerebral palsy; wheelchair; very mild speech impediment that manifests itself in a kind of halted way of speaking; otherwise, determinedly polished.

SETTING

John's accessible bedroom.

TIME

Present day.

AUTHOR'S NOTES

Specific ages don't matter as much, as long as they're both about the same age.

Dialogistics:

// indicate overlap

... indicate active pauses and silences

ABOUT THE PLAYWRIGHT

Martyna Majok was born in Bytom, Poland, and aged in Jersey and Chicago. Her plays include *Ironbound, Petty Harbour, reWilding, Women at the Well, Mouse in a Jar,* and *the friendship of her thighs.* Martyna's work has been seen and developed at Steppenwolf Theatre Company, Marin Theatre Company, Actors Theatre of Louisville, The John F. Kennedy Center, The Satori Group, New York Stage & Film, the claque, Yale Cabaret, The Playwright and Director Center of Moscow, Round House Theatre, Rep Tape Theatre, and The LIDA Project, among others. Martyna has been awarded The David Calicchio Emerging American Playwright Prize, The 2050 Fellowship from New York Theatre Workshop, Aurora Theatre's Global Age Project Prize, The National New Play Network Smith Prize for Political Playwriting, The Jane Chambers Student Feminist Playwriting Prize, The Merage Fellowship for the American Dream, The Olga and Paul Menn Award in Playwriting, a Ragdale residency, The Howard Stein Scholarship for Playwriting, commissions from EST/Sloan Foundation, Walkabout Theatre, and The Foundry Theatre, and publications by Samuel French and Smith & Kraus. BA: University of Chicago; MFA: Yale School of Drama. She has taught playwriting at Wesleyan, The New Haven Co-Op High School, New Jersey Repertory Company, and SUNY Purchase, and assisted Paula Vogel at Yale. She is developing a musical about modern day Chernobyl for The Foundry Theatre. Proud member of Ensemble Studio Theatre's Youngblood, The Women's Project Lab, and Ars Nova's Uncharted. Martyna was the 2012-2013 NNPN playwright-in-residence at New Jersey Repertory Company. She lives in Queens and her last name is pronounced "MY-oak," in case you were wondering.

Part One

*(Early morning. A bedroom. **JESS** stands alone, a bit nervous. She wears a hoodie and jeans/sweats.)*

JESS. Does it always – ?

JOHN. *(off)* Hold on.

JESS. It always take this long?

JOHN. *(off)* Can't hear you.

JESS. Sorry. Is there somethin else you want me to do? While you're –

(Flush, offstage.)

*(**JOHN** enters in a wheelchair.)*

I don't wanna take advantage of the hourly rate. Not, y'know, doin anything while yer, in there.

JOHN. Do you have a problem being alone?

JESS. …

JOHN. You'll get to think a lot. Waiting's
part of the job.

JESS. Sorry. I never worked with the, Differently-Abled –

JOHN. Don't do that.

JESS. What?

JOHN. Don't call it that.

JESS. Why, I –

JOHN. Don't call it different
-ly-abled.

JESS. Is that not the right term?

JOHN. It's
fucking retarded.

JESS. So what do I, how do I, *refer* to you?
JOHN. Are you planning on
     talking about me?
JESS. No.
JOHN. Why not?
     I'm very interesting.
     …
JESS. So after you, y'know, then I –?
JOHN. Why do you want
     this job?
JESS. I thought,
     the experience and I –, it'd be –
JOHN. Why do you want –
JESS. The money.
JOHN. Good.
JESS. And I'd be good at it. I'm
     responsible.
JOHN. Good. So you won't
     lose me.
     Have you ever washed someone before?
JESS. *(lying)* Yup!
JOHN. How much can you lift? Think you can
     lift me?
JESS. …
JOHN. 155 pounds.
     Wet.
JESS. I can lift you.
JOHN. You won't be
     bench-pressing me. You lift me out of my chair, then
     help me onto my
     shower seat. We do it fast. You wash me. My
     hair. Teeth. Trim my
     whiskers.

You keep me handsome.

I'll teach you.

(**JOHN** *reaches a shaky hand into his pocket.*)

(*He pulls out a crumbled paper, smoothes it out on his thighs. Looks at it. Judges.*)

JESS. Whatever I can't do, I'll get better.

(*Looks at her.*)

JOHN. You went here?

JESS. Yeah.

...

Why wouldn't I.

JOHN. ...

JESS. And you're here for –?

JOHN. PhD.
Political
Science. Just moved here.
From *Cambridge.*

JESS. Harvard?

JOHN. Since you
mention it.

(**JOHN** *judges the resume.*)

JESS. Whatever I can't do, I'll figure it out.

(*He looks up from the resume.*)

JOHN. Jess.

JESS. Yeah?

JOHN. -ica?

JESS. Just Jess.

JOHN. Early riser, *Jess?*

JESS. Can be.

JOHN. 6am?

JESS. *(lying)* Yup!

JOHN. Well then

(He extends his hand out to her. A moment. She watches it shake. Then she shakes his hand.)

Here

we go.

***

Part Two

(One month later. A groove and a comfort has been established.)

*(Throughout this, **JESS** showers **JOHN**. This involves helping lift him from his wheelchair onto his shower seat, undressing him completely, washing his hair, soaping his body and rinsing him off. This can be staged with a chair and a bucket of water.)*

JESS. I mean I don't love these women either – sometimes they're worse than that but I'm not givin the girl tequila when she's that fuckin *done*, y'know.

JOHN. Naturally.

JESS. Especially when she ain't order it. I mean I'll take a man's money whatever but No Rapes on my watch. This girl's on the couches we got, in the back, right, half dressed, half asleep (and this place is not, y'know, it's *loud*), and this guy to me he's like, 'Yo. cmere'. Like 'Ey-oh!, OVER HERE'. And he's one of those, y'know, with the button doooown –

JOHN. Right.

JESS. – jeeeeans –

JOHN. *(judgment)* God.

JESS. – with the hair, y'know what I'm sayin?

JOHN. Oh yes.

JESS. And orange. He tans. And he's like 'This girl needs a *shot*.' So I'm like 'Listen Chief I think she's *good*'. And he's like 'Listen bitch –'

JOHN. Uh-oh.

JESS. 'Who's got the money', he says, 'and who the fuck are you?'

JOHN. *(gasps)*

JESS. And he throws this balled up napkin in my face.

JOHN. Some people.

JESS. Bouncer palmed his greasy head and threw his douche ass out.

JOHN. Good.

JESS. Man, fuck rich people. No offense but, heads on sticks. France should happen here.

(*A moment of silent showering.*)

I don't know why people gotta judge you by yer job. I'm not my job.

JOHN. People have to judge you by something.

JESS. Except no the fucks don't.

JOHN. How else will they know if they're
winning or not?

JESS. I don't judge people.

JOHN. (*makes a judgmental noise*)

JESS. I make a sincere effort not to judge people.

JOHN. Well I hope you never drown.

JESS. I hope you never drown too, John.

JOHN. Because if it's you and I and Michael
Phelps in the
Hamptons and you get a cramp? And you call on
me because you're not judgmental? I do believe you'd
likely
die.
...
I judged you.

JESS. How'd you judge me? Here, you want yer – (*wash cloth*)

JOHN. Yes please, here –

(*JESS puts into JOHN's hand a soaped up wash cloth.*)

JESS. Got it?

JOHN. Got it, thanks.

(*He uses this to wash his privates. JESS turns away so he can have privacy. It's not awkward. Routine.*)

JESS. How'd you judge me?

JOHN. Well.

    I judged you well, I think.

    You haven't

    lost me.

    (He drops the cloth on the shower floor – he's done with it. She rinses him. She lifts him from his shower seat on his wheelchair seat. Dries his body.)

JESS. You barely leave.

JOHN. I leave.

JESS. To class yeah. I never see you out.

JOHN. Big city.

JESS. In the neighborhood, even. Never see you.

JOHN. Well

    I never see you.

JESS. I don't go out much.

JOHN. At all.

JESS. So how did you judge me?

    Polo or V-neck?

JOHN. Crew, please.

    That olive one there.

    (She dresses him.)

JESS. Nice. Is this new?

JOHN. I may have even *gone out* for it.

JESS. So how did –?

JOHN. Your body.

    For one.

    Whether you can

    lift me.

JESS. Sure

JOHN. Your degree.

JESS. English?

JOHN. Means you'll

    conversate.

JESS. And

JOHN. Why don't you
go out?

JESS. Much

JOHN. At all. Why not? Someone like
you?
…

JESS. *(knows what he means)* Someone like
what, John?

JOHN. *(knows she knows what he means)* And because you
went here. Was another way I judged you.
It means you're not a
dumbass.

JESS. Yer not gonna say it, are you.

JOHN. Fuck nope, Jess. Quite right. Fuck nope.

(**JOHN** *should be dressed by now.* **JESS** *is taking in her*
work.)

How do I look?

JESS. Good.

JOHN. Good.
…
Good.

JESS. *(preparing to leave)* Okay, well if –

JOHN. Are you around Friday night?

JESS. Am I, around?

JOHN. This
Friday night?

JESS. Tomorrow?

JOHN. I know it's late notice.

JESS. No it's –

JOHN. Would you want to come
over?
…

JESS. Here?

JOHN. At seven?

JESS. You don't usually ask me to come by at night.

JOHN. I know.

JESS. And on a *Friday* night

JOHN. I know it's late –

JESS. Yes.

> …

JOHN. Oh,

> my, you work, don't you?, at the,
>
> //other–

JESS. That's okay. Someone'll cover.

JOHN. Are you sure?

JESS. Yes.

> Yeah.
>
> Love to.

JOHN. Good.

JESS. Good.

> …

JOHN. Cool.

> *(She wipes some saliva that has collected on his mouth, carefully.)*

JESS. Cool.

> *(And exits. With a little sass in her step.)*

***

Part Three

(Friday evening.)

(Nice lighting. Music plays. Something like Tom Waits' "I Can't Wait to Get Off Work (And See My Baby).")

*(**JESS** enters. She's dressed up. Lookin good. Feelin good. She carries a black plastic shopping bag. Sets it down. She takes in the music and mood-lighting. Nice job, Tiger.)*

JESS. John?

(Flush, offstage.)

JOHN. *(off)* You're
early.

*(**JOHN** enters.)*

You're dressed so –

JESS. Yeah.

JOHN. Nice.

JESS. Well, you only see me in the mornings.

JOHN. You look nice.

…

I'm gonna need a
shower and //you're all –

JESS. Oh yeah?

JOHN. And a shave.

JESS. *(She's into it.)* Okay.

JOHN. I know this is a bit
different
from our usual –

JESS. Uh-huh.

JOHN. That's why I asked you over. I wanted an extra good
shave.

JESS. I can do that.

JOHN. I thought if it was too early, like

early in the week or this morning, if you shaved me
    too early,
I'd be prickly.

JESS. That's considerate.

JOHN. That's why I
    asked you over. And...

JESS. Uh-huh...

JOHN. And I'm nervous.

JESS. You don't hafta be nervous.

JOHN. I've never
    done this before.

JESS. You don't hafta be nervous.

JOHN. I've considered hookers.

JESS. You don't need to do that.

JOHN. This is not a very manly conversation. I thought
    when I spoke of hookers it would be manly.

JESS. Don't talk about hookers.

JOHN. And I just didn't know where to start looking
    for – God, another unmanly, I simply shouldn't ever
    talk about hookers.

JESS. No.

JOHN. But if we don't talk about how far we've come, Jess,
    not doing certain things, how will anyone know how
    far we've come?

JESS. What do you wanna do first?

JOHN. Cry my God I'm so nervous.

JESS. Don't cry.

JOHN. And also laugh! Like jump! My skin wants to
    jump! I feel like I could
        WOO!

JESS. I could shave you first.

JOHN. Good plan.

JESS. Then shower.

JOHN. Yes.

JESS. So the cream, the –

JOHN. Right. Good.

JESS. – will take care of itself.

JOHN. Do we have time for both?

JESS. Absolutely.

JOHN. I'm meeting her at 8.

   …

JESS. Excuse me?

JOHN. *(in his own world)* Mm. What time is Maybe I should
   skip one. If I had to skip one, shower or
   shave: which?

JESS. For a…

JOHN. First date!

JESS. With a…

JESS. Hooker?   JOHN. Graduate student!

JOHN. Madelyn!
   From *Oxford*!
   PhD with a focus in *Hume,*
   the minx.
   At 8!
   Just like her figure.
   Oh!
   How do you *do* this? How do you even
   do this?
   What if she doesn't – well I imagine she
   does or she wouldn't – But what if I –
   And what if she –
   Oh how do you –
   Jess!
   How does this work? How does this crazy thing that is
   people
   work?

   (Amidst this, while JOHN *is oblivious,* JESS *has taken
   from her plastic bag a bottle of wine. Opens it. A twist
   off. Pours a glass.)*

JOHN. What is this?

JESS. Pinot.

(She puts a straw in his glass.)

JOHN. Good idea.

(He drinks from the straw. And wonders.)

Oh Jess.

Jess Jess.

How do you do it?

JESS. You'll be great.

(She drinks from the bottle.)

Shave and a shower?

JOHN. Shave and a shower, yes.

Please.

Thank you.

(He dreams of Madelyn.)

Yes!

*(**JESS**. goes off for the supplies.)*

(On her way, she turns up the music. It swells.)

End of Play

The Logic

Will Arbery

THE LOGIC was first produced as part of the Theater Masters National MFA Festival (Julia Hansen, Artistic Director) on February 2, 2014 at The Aspen Institute/Aspen High School in Aspen, Colorado. It was directed by Stephen Cedars, produced by Naomi McDougall Jones, and associate produced by Ariana Paganetti. The scenic designer was Tom Ward and technical director was Brett Maughan. The Production Stage Manager was Mark Hoffner. The cast was as follows:

EVAN . . . . Sean Warnecke

ANDREW . . . . John Rios

THE LOGIC was produced again at the American Theater of Actors in New York City on April 22, 2014. The producing team was the same, and the actors were:

EVAN . . . . David Meyers

ANDREW . . . . Patrick Ball

THE LOGIC was produced as part of the Samuel French Off Off Broadway Short Play Festival at the Peter J. Sharp Theatre, Playwrights Horizons in New York City on August 8, 2014. It was directed by Knud Adams. The cast was as follows:

EVAN . . . . Sam Alper

ANDREW . . . . David Rosenblatt

CHARACTERS

EVAN – 24, New York-based writer
ANDREW – 24, Texas-based inmate

SETTING

Facebook chat.

TIME

The course of a few months, this year.

AUTHOR'S NOTE

One of the challenges of this production is how to stage a digital interaction. Directors should take advantage of the freedom this script allows them, but my strong belief is that the most effective way to stage this is to eliminate the use of computers or phones as props, and to create a highly minimalized and artful theatrical space. In the OOB Festival production, the director solved this problem by having them sit at tables next to each other and face out towards the audience. They were illuminated only by two small white lights, which sat on the desk and illuminated their faces. He also solved some blocking problems in especially effective ways: Andrew doing push-ups during the transitions and covering his face with his shirt during the book excerpt, for example. Also, during the shorter scenes, he underscored the dialogue with music by Krzysztof Penderecki, which worked very well.

SPECIAL THANKS

I have so much gratitude for Knud, David, and Sam for their wonderful production.

The most help I received on the script was from Stephen Cedars, who directed it for the Theater Masters festival in Aspen and New York. He understood the soul of the play on a deep level, and I can't thank him enough. Additional thanks: Naomi McDougall-Jones, Julia Hansen, Robert LuPone, and Andrew Leynse. I also learned a lot about the show from a series of stagings/readings, and I'm indebted to Ryan Drake, Chris Stevens, and Eamon Levesque at Kenyon College; Tommy Rivera-Vega, Jessie David Perez and Juan Castañeda at Late Night Teatro Vista; Josh Bywater and Alex Benjamin at Living Room Playmakers.

ABOUT THE PLAYWRIGHT

Will Arbery is a playwright, performer, writer and filmmaker. As a playwright, he's enjoyed experiences at Dixon Place, Chicago Dramatists, Calliope Theater Company, Theater Masters, Samuel French, Hearth Gods, Teatro Vista, iDiOM Theater, Living Room Playmakers, Tiny Rhino, and #serials@theflea. His play *We Were Nothing!* was produced site-specifically in New York. He's a collaborator with boomerang dance. His writing has been published by *Better: Culture and Lit, Word Riot, decomP, The Awl, Howl Round, D Magazine,* and more. Currently, he's completing several short films, and studying towards an MFA in Writing for the Screen and Stage at Northwestern. He grew up in Dallas, Texas, the only boy with seven sisters.

(**ANDREW** *and* **EVAN** *sit near each other. The stage is mostly dark, and despite their proximity, the mood is lonely.*)

ANDREW. Hey Evan. Its me. Devil kid. Back from the dead.

(Pause.)

We made a porn together. Ring a bell?

EVAN. Hahahaha wow Andrew man
First of all
We never made it. We couldn't find a girl

ANDREW. Nah it's true we woulda been arrest anyway
Arrested

EVAN. We were kids they wouldn't have arrested us

ANDREW. Haha

EVAN. Haha
Andrew man what's up

ANDREW. Haha been a while dude

EVAN. Yeah I was surprised when you friended me
I mean not surprised
Just I thought wow it's really been a while

ANDREW. Haha yeah

EVAN. Since what 6th grade

ANDREW. Summer after 6th when I moved to fucken Midlothian

EVAN. 12 years

ANDREW. I guess. Shit. Haha

EVAN. Haha

ANDREW. So what are you up to

EVAN. Ahhhh I dunno
Working for a literary agency
Doing book stuff reading books all day. Books books books

ANDREW. Fuck yeah
　　Remember when we had that plan
　　I was gonna be a horror writer man, Stephen King
　　league
　　You were gonna be my agent
　　Do you remember that
　　We had a plan

EVAN. Yeah

ANDREW. What kind of stuff do you do there

EVAN. I mean I'm low man, low on the ladder
　　I'm just like an assistant
　　It's a job

ANDREW. Wanna hear about a dream I had

EVAN. Sure

　　(Pause.)

　　"Andrew is typing…" haha

　　(Pause.)

　　What are you typing, a novel

ANDREW. I've been having these dreams where im back at
school and suddenly the whole world is fucking every
man for himself, u know? All the guys from school are
trying to kill each other man and I'm fukken king of
the hunt, I'm slicing all those guys up, but the one
I'm looking for is you, because I want to protect you.
But when I find you man I see you and I pickup this
special gun, my gun, it shoots hundreds of exacto-
knife blades into people's body, all over their body.
I find you and you stand there looking at me and I
shoot you. I feel bad about it but I shoot you. Because
I don't know you anymore and maybe you aren't so
gentle anymore, maybe you can kill me. But then
suddenly I'm you and I feel all the blades in my body,
in my veins, in my temple, slicing through nerves and
I stumble around and I'm you I'm you and it hurts so
bad but the pain doesn't know where to go so I get

all numb and then I have this thought "this is what it's like, this is what it's like to die, I'm dying, this is it, there's no escaping it, any second now I'll die, any second, any second," and I stumble and lie down and wake up.

EVAN. Whoa. You were me

ANDREW. I dream about being you a lot haha

Anyway just a crazy dream I guess but I love that shit

EVAN. Yeah

ANDREW. That dark shit

EVAN. Fuck yeah

ANDREW. I always did man…

EVAN. So what are you doing are you playing basketball?

Are you married?

Are you skinny are you fat?

You look skinny as hell in your pictures but there's only like 4 of them.

ANDREW. Hahahah no what the fuck. Married?

The future's easy

To predict

EVAN. What do you mean

ANDREW. Think about it

EVAN. …tell me

ANDREW. There's a logic to the way we each ended up

I'm not just unlucky, I recognize that fully

I always wanted to be a writer

Real bad

But like

My brain was too fucking juiced. Too scary

There's a logic why I'm where I am and you're where you are

But that's why we had the plan

EVAN. What are you doing man

Where are you even living

ANDREW. I'm in Texas man

Still

EVAN. Cool

How is it

ANDREW. haha

I gotta go, I only get 10 minutes on here

EVAN. On where

ANDREW. The internet

EVAN. Oh

Why

ANDREW. Penitentiary man

Rules

They monitor this shit

Whatever peace brother

I knew you were working in books brother, that's why I found you. I'm glad I found you

(**ANDREW** *stands up and leaves his chair. He does something physical to indicate the passage of time.*)

EVAN. Shit man

Really?

I didn't know you'd been arrested.

(*Pause.*)

You gone?

What'd you do?

Tell me what you did

(*Pause.* **EVAN** *changes a shirt.* **ANDREW** *comes back, sits down. Now it's night.*)

ANDREW. Evan.

Evan.

Evan man.

You there?

I have something to ask you.

(*Pause.*)

Fuck dude why sign on if you're not gonna be on.

10 mins are up

(Pause.)

Well I wrote a book.

*(Pause. **ANDREW** stands up, leaves the chair. Does something physical to indicate the passage of time. **EVAN** finally engages.)*

EVAN. Hey im here.

You still theeeeeeeeeeeeeere?

Sorry im drunk

Oh shit you sent me your book

120 pages nice. Doable. So many books area lie

are like*

infinite

Hahahaha watch this

Do they let you watch shit

Ugh I've been spending way too much money

New york's really hard

Are you gone

Been thinkin about you latelay

Late lay hahaha

*(Pause. **EVAN** changes shirts. **ANDREW** returns.)*

ANDREW. Did you read the book?

EVAN. No I haven't had a chance yet. I've been pretty busy but I'll check it out right now.

ANDREW. Okay.

(Pause.)

Thoughts?

EVAN. Can't read that fast

ANDREW. Word

(Pause.)

If you're at the part where the main character beats his grandmother's head in, that's based on a dream I had where my nana was a zombie.

Yes I laughed while I was beating her and my mom
laughed too
That's just straight out of the dream man
But come on man this is a great fucken line:
"Nana was the generational ground I walked on, and
now her guts and brains were the literal ground, and I
walked on them." That's a great fucken line.

(Pause.)

Remember when we would go camping at my lake
house
Remember when I made you watch porno
You freaked out man.

EVAN. Your little brother was there
   That's why I freaked out

ANDREW. You were a pussy about it
   Colin was chill with it

EVAN. He was 7

ANDREW. w/e

EVAN. Haha
   Yeah

ANDREW. You watch porn now or are you still a gaylord

   (Pause.)

   I guess u r gaylord

EVAN. I watch porn

ANDREW. Nice.
   This chick won't stop messaging me
   She's all concerned
   I'm like shut up

   (Pause.)

   Time's running out here
   My man
   My man my man
   We could still do the plan

It's working out
The plan is working out

(Pause. **ANDREW** *stands, moves away.* **EVAN** *takes off his shirt and sits shirtless for the rest of the play.* **ANDREW** *returns, sits down. During the scene,* **EVAN** *does something a guy alone in his room would do.)*

EVAN. I read your book.

ANDREW. fuckin brilliant

Amirite

I think about you all the time I feel like this is some good shit

EVAN. Yeah

I wish we could hang out in person

Have you stalked me at all, like looked at my pictures

ANDREW. Nah

EVAN. Cool just wondering. I look like less of a dork now.
Jesus this book

ANDREW. What

This book what

(Pause.)

If you could help out, try to get that published
That would be awesome

(Pause.)

Do you remember when I used to blow shit up
Do you remember when I used to masturbate during class
I said I was itchin for ants
I was jerking off in class though
& u kept my secret
I robbed a car in the fuckin suburbs and shot a man in gym shorts
He was going to the gym

(Pause.)

Can't wait to hear your brilliant constructive criticism,
Evan

(*Pause.*)

Are you weirded out about the you stuff.

EVAN. A little, yeah

ANDREW. Why

EVAN. You kill me

"It was time to die. By dying live, by living die. I took a
deep breath and shot Evan in the face."

ANDREW. As an act of mercy

EVAN. How is that

An act of mercy

ANDREW. If I have to explain that to you

You aren't as smart as I thought

Examine the text Gaylord

EVAN. I gotta go dude but

ANDREW. No I gotta go

I die a week from Friday

No more internetz

EVAN. Are you serious

ANDREW. Mebbe

Mebbe not

EVAN. What

ANDREW. Miss you bro

Try to get that thing on the fuckin stands man

Get that book on the fuckin charts

On the lists

Oprah's book club

Get it into hands my man

Freak out America

Nah the world

Fuck em up show em a real fucking human being

Get rich off me I don't give a fuck

I just want to stick it to logic for once motherfucker
I want to talk from the dead and prove every
motherfucker wrong
Yeah makes sense
For you and me right
Logical choice for both of us, yeah

EVAN. Andrew

ANDREW. I could try to go back in time but man things
just work out the way they work out. Fuck it all makes
sense. I see it all fit together.
But I hate that.
That's the way my brain is man, it's either logic or
fucking nightmare.
s.
nightmares.
Ok time up for real, they're yelling
Being a little lenient though since like
I'm fucked anyway
See ya

EVAN. Are you serious Andrew
It says you're still on.
Are you still on
When you get back
Or I mean when we talk again
I'd love to talk to you about this. It's rough at times
For me to read
But there are some parts:

(**EVAN** *reads.*)

"It started with the neck, just a swelling sensation.
Then it sort of became this feeling of being choked,
from the outside. I feel it now. I felt it all day yesterday.
I think I might have felt it the day I was born. I think
I might have felt it inside my mother's womb. And
I certainly felt it now. Someone was choking me.
Someone was telling me what to do. "Man, it's scary

feeling like there's no escape from your own mind," I said, looking down at Evan, who was breathing hard. "What's going to happen? I am sure that something terrible will happen." I sat on top of him and pointed the gun down. There, I felt everything come back, like a bunch of bullets of memory, and everything hurt as much as a bullet. But instead of putting holes in my body, they filled me with every good thing I ever did, and every good thing anyone ever did to me. My arms and legs and head and chest were full of rides home and giving the homeless dude at 7-11 some money and notes in my lunch from my mom and staying up all night talking to someone freaked out. But then it stopped, and I looked down at my friend's peaceful face. It was much easier not to be afraid with Evan. I didn't know how to fail with him. But time causes failure just as it causes success. It was time to die. By dying live, by living die."

(Pause.)

Like you could have changed my name
But there's something to it. I'd love to work with you on it if you can. I'd love to do the plan

(**ANDREW** *walks off stage.*)

Okay you're gone
Well since you can't see it
I used to have a huge crush on you
Haha

(Pause.)

Oh shit does this go into your inbox anyway
Fuck I'm sorry man aghh fuck sorry
delete it

(Longer pause.)

Talk to you in what
12 years
maybe

(**EVAN** *sits silent and alone. End of play.*)

Mandate

Kelly Younger

MANDATE received its premiere production at the Stella Adler Theatre in Hollywood, California for *Snapshots: A Theatrical Benefit,* produced by Nicki Georgi and Lara Wickes. It was directed by the playwright. The cast was as follows:

DREW . . . . Drew Powell

MARC . . . . Marc Valera

MANDATE was produced as part of the Samuel French Off Off Broadway Short Play Festival at the Peter J. Sharp Theatre, Playwrights Horizons in New York City on August 8, 2014. The performance was directed by the playwright. The cast was as follows:

DREW . . . . Drew Powell

MARC . . . . Marc Valera

CHARACTERS

DREW – male, mid-late 30s, big, pudgy, heart on his sleeve.
MARC – male, mid-late 30s, short, thin, buttoned up.

SETTING

A crowded sports bar.

PROPERTY PLOT

Bar table.
Two bar stools.
Two mugs of beer.
One bowl of peanuts.
Hello Kitty notepad and pencil.

COSTUMES

DREW – Sweatpants, t-shirt, sweatshirt. Soft and comfortable. Think less what a guy would wear to the gym and more what a mom might wear to the park. It's coordinated. He probably thought *a lot* about what he was going to wear.

MARC – Khakis, white collared shirt, plain sweater vest. Pressed and tucked in. Sensible shoes. He probably has a closet filled with nothing but this outfit.

AUTHOR'S NOTE

This play is dedicated to Drew and Marc (aka, The Charm Offensive).

ABOUT THE PLAYWRIGHT

Kelly Younger's plays have been staged Off Broadway at Irish Repertory Theatre and Manhattan Theatre Club, and regionally at The Firehouse Theatre, Bloomington Playwrights Project, Naked Angels, Furious Theatre Company, Gloucester Stage Company, Pacific Residents Theatre, Ensemble Studio Theatre/LA, The Blank Theatre, and Orlando Shakespeare Theatre, and internationally in Dublin, London, Canada, Dubai, and the Edinburgh Fringe Festival. He is the winner of The Firehouse Theatre Festival of New American Plays, the Riva Shriner Comedy Award, the John Gassner New Play Award, and has been a finalist for the Heidemann Award at The Actors Theatre of Louisville, the Academy of Motion Picture Arts and Sciences Nicholl Fellowship, the Warner Brothers television writing fellowship, the Paul Newman & Joanne Woodward Drama Prize, the Laurents/Hatcher Award, and a nominee for the IRNE award for Best New Play. His plays have been published by Playscripts and Smith & Kraus, and he is a frequent participant in the Last Frontier Theatre Conference. Younger is a proud member of The Dramatists Guild of America and of Pacific Residents Theatre in Los Angeles. Younger is managed by Bruce Miller at Washington Square Arts and Films in NY and is represented by Seth Glewen at The Gersh Agency. More info at www.KellyYounger.com.

(In darkness. Sounds of erotic grunting and panting.)

DREW. C'mon! Give it to me!

*(Lights up on **DREW** giving the Heimlich to **MARC**.)*

You can do it!

*(**MARC** launches the peanut from his mouth.)*

There it is!

*(Beat. **DREW** acknowledges the unseen bar patrons with a big grin. **MARC** is horrified.)*

MARC. What the hell dude?

DREW. You're welcome.

MARC. I wasn't choking.

DREW. Sure you were.

MARC. I was eating a peanut.

DREW. That got lodged in your throat.

MARC. Not until you started crushing my lungs.

DREW. Wait, seriously? You weren't choking?

MARC. That's what I was trying to say but you were shouting and thrusting and Christ, where did you learn the Heimlich, prison?

DREW. *(hands to throat)* You gave the universal sign for choking.

MARC. I was just adjusting my collar. I told you I was coming to the bar straight from a haircut.

DREW. Oh. Itchy?

MARC. Yeah.

DREW. Well it looks good.

MARC. Thanks?

DREW. Guess that was pretty awkward.

MARC. Really awkward.

DREW. But you're fit, man.

> *(poking him)* Could feel a pretty tight little core while I was squeezing you.

MARC. Not any less awkward.

DREW. I put on some sympathy weight when Hillary first got pregnant with Addison. She used to say we were having twins. One in her belly, one in mine. Then when we had Bridgie I was like, bring on the sweatpants!

> *(**MARC** lifts his beer, **DREW** quickly follows and over-eagerly cheers him, nearly smashing his mug.)*

> *(singing)*

> HERE'S TO GOOD FRIENDS. TONIGHT IS KIND OF SPECIAL.

> *(**MARC** doesn't really know how to respond.)*

MARC. So, Beth told me you're a teacher.

DREW. Earth science and driver's ed. 124 kids. All-girls school.

MARC. All girls. That's a lot.

DREW. Don't have to tell me. But I can text 90 words in 2 minutes 26 seconds, so, you know, I'm kind of a popular teacher. And I know the words to every One Direction song. Go on. Try me.

MARC. With what?

DREW. One Direction challenge.

MARC. I don't know what that is.

DREW. Seriously? They're like the freaking Monkees for the new generation.

> *(bursts into song* and boy-band gestures)*

> YOU DON'T KNOW YOU'RE BEAUTIFUL! OH OH! THAT'S WHAT MAKES YOU BEAUTIFUL!

MARC. *(cutting him off)* Jake's kind of more into *Star Wars*.

DREW. Ah, man. I'd give anything to have a son. Don't get me wrong. I love my girls. I'm just, you know, kind of outnumbered. I brought out all my old action figures and the girls just wanted to have a pool party with Barbie. I was like, Boba Fett does not swim!

---

* See Music Use Note (p.3)

MARC. I do this funny thing with Jake, whenever we go through the security gate at our condo, it opens automatically, but I put my hand up like a Jedi and act like I'm giving it a force push, and when it opens, you should see his face.

DREW. *(with deep admiration)* You're amazing.

MARC. I'm sure you do loads of stuff like that.

DREW. Addison and Bridgie paint my toe nails. In fact, my toe nails are always painted. Wanna see?

MARC. I'm good.

(Awkward moment.)

DREW. Can I tell you a secret?

MARC. I think you just did.

DREW. I'm a Brony.

MARC. A what?

DREW. A bro who likes *My Little Pony.*

MARC. That's a thing?

DREW. Huge. My girls got me hooked. We threw a party for the coronation episode where Princess Celestia finally gave Twilight Sparkle her wings. Man. That was a great night.

(beat)

Friendship *is* magic.

*(**MARC** takes a deep drink. **DREW** mirrors his every move.)*

This is nice. I'm really glad our wives set this up.

MARC. Yeah. Can't wait to thank her.

DREW. They totally knew we'd get along. And it's so hard, you know, with work and kids and everything, I mean, how do people even make friends any more? Especially guys, you know? Like there's no way guys just become friends like you did in college. Had a class together or in a frat or something. Now it's all about do the spouses get along, and what if they do but their kid is an asshole or the kids get along but the parents are assholes and do you want to be best friends?

MARC. *(beat)* What's that?

DREW. Do you want to be my best friend?

MARC. *(laughs, stops)* You serious?

DREW. I mean, like, unless you've already got one. Do you?

MARC. A best friend?

DREW. And wives don't count. I'm talking guy best friends. You already have one?

MARC. Dude. I haven't really thought about it like that since…

DREW. Since what?

MARC. Grade school.

DREW. So do ya?

MARC. I've got plenty of friends.

DREW. Not counting work.

MARC. Ok, yeah.

DREW. And not counting dads from your kid's school.

MARC. Ok. Yeah, still got 'em.

DREW. And not counting guys from college.

MARC. Ok.

DREW. Or facebook.

MARC. Well who's left?

DREW. See?

MARC. You basically eliminated all my social circles.

DREW. Hillary's got like ten best girlfriends and they go out and talk on the phone every day and confide in one another and talk about work and yoga and how their bodies are changing and does Beth still give you blow jobs?

MARC. Dude!

DREW. Because before we were married Hillary treated me like a popsicle on the Fourth of July but now I'm lucky to get one on my birthday. And this is what guys should talk about, right?

MARC. No.

DREW. But our wives do all the time about everything and
I mean *everything* like shopping and gossip and your
yeast infection.

MARC. WHAT THE FUCK!

(looking around)

You know about that?

(angry)

And it was not a yeast infection.

(adjusting his crotch)

It was a fungus.

DREW. Made of yeast. Don't be embarrassed bro, it
happens. You just gotta wash better after the gym.

MARC. Dude. I don't need your hygiene advice.

DREW. Mmmmm-apparently you do, 'cause where do you
think she heard about soaking the boys in vinegar? It's
the only cure for when your balls start baking bread.

(patting him a little too high on the thigh)

You're welcome.

MARC. Can we please just watch the game?

DREW. Oh. Are we moving too fast? Or you already have a
best friend?

MARC. No. I mean, yeah… that's right, I do.

DREW. Who?

MARC. The best man at our wedding. JD. He lives in
Baltimore now.

DREW. How often do you guys talk?

MARC. Enough. I guess.

DREW. Like, once a week, or what?

MARC. Like… I don't know. I guess – When was the last
time I talked to him?

DREW. See? He was your best man and you don't even talk
anymore.

MARC. We don't have to. He's the kind of guy that just, you know, we don't need to talk a lot.

DREW. I'm not like that. And I don't think most guys are either, we just think we're supposed to act that way.

MARC. Didn't you have a best man?

DREW. Hillary's brother. He doesn't like me all that much. Thinks I come on too strong.

MARC. Look, Drake.

DREW. Drew.

MARC. Sorry. Drew. Listen, Beth told me her friend from yoga… your wife… had a cool husband and we should meet up for a beer and I said, ok, sure, thinking we would just, you know, meet up for a beer, but, all this best friends forever kinda thing is just a little… I'm just not really… in the market for one, you know?

DREW. *(beat)* That's cool.

MARC. Let's just drink our beers, watch the game, be guys. In silence.

*(****DREW**** plays it off. They both watch the game. Then **DREW** slowly reaches into his pocket, slyly pulls out a Hello Kitty note pad, flips the pink pages, lifts his pen, and scratches something out.)*

What's that?

(grabbing the pad)

Did you just cross my name off of some… list? What is this?

(He flips through pages. Clearly a long list.)

"Possible candidates for my new best friend." How many… I'm at the bottom? Dave Scales is on here? That guy's a tool. How is he higher up on the list than me?

DREW. What's it matter now? I've run out of names.

MARC. Wait, seriously, you've done *this* with all these guys?

DREW. And none of them ever called for a second date.

MARC. Maybe because you're calling it a date.

DREW. What would you call it?

MARC. Just… hanging out. Grabbing a drink. Getting to know each other. Kind of like… kind of like… yeah, I guess…

(stands, pulls out wallet)

Look! You seem like a great guy.

DREW. Here we go again.

MARC. But it's not really a great time for me, right now, and I…

*(**DREW** tries to keep it together, but it's no use.)*

Wha – what's happening?

(The tears are flowing.)

You ok? Hey. Buddy.

DREW. *(through snot)* I'm not your buddy. You've made *that* perfectly clear.

MARC. Woah. Seriously, pal.

DREW. *(losing it)* I'm not your pal either. Or your *amigo*. Or your *dawg*. Or Edgar Allen *Bro*. I used to be fun. I lived my life by the 5 Bs. Beer. Bros. Babes. Ball. And Buffett. Guys used to kill to hang out with me. But now I'm on freakin' list-serves with mommy and me groups. I have contact info for three different lactation consultants. The last sporting event I went to was a sale at American Girl. I've become this over-weight, pathetic, whiskered marshmallow! I don't know how to find my balls.

(crossing to him)

You gotta help me! I took care of your balls now it's your turn with my balls!

*(**DREW** collapses into **MARC** like a blubbering mess.)*

MARC. *(embarrassed, trapped)* There there.

*(Then **MARC** pats him with sincerity, gently holding the big lug.)*

Hey. It's ok. It's going to be ok.

*(**DREW** eventually pulls himself together, embarrassed, patting under his eyes with his ring fingers.)*

DREW. Ok. I'm ok. I'm all right.

MARC. Look, man. I get it.

DREW. You're just saying that because I snotted on your sweater vest.

MARC. No, seriously. I do. I mean. If you asked me in high school if I would even be the kind of guy who wore sweater vests, I would have laughed right in your face. You think I wanted to grow up and be this sorry ass cubicle jockey who works sixty hours a week pushing numbers around? You want to hear something sad? The only thing I excel at... is Excel. I make good spreadsheets. That's it. And my life has become this massive, over-organized spreadsheet with cells that just go on and on and on. It never ends. And it's sucking the life out of me, one *spread-shit* at a time. Damnit. You're gonna make me cry now.

DREW. It's ok. Spreadsheets are hard.

MARC. They're *really* hard!

DREW. But it feels better to talk about, doesn't it.

*(A moment. **MARC** nods, takes his seat.)*

MARC. Look. I don't have a lot of time right now, with work and the kids and all, and, I don't know if I'm like best friend material here or anything but... you can keep my name on the list... if you want. And I'll... you know... I'll call you... for a second, you know, whatever this is. And maybe we can try it again. See where it goes. Cool?

DREW. Cool.

*(They both stare forward in silence, watching the game. Slowly, wonderfully, a big, delighted grin grows across **DREW***'s face.)*

We totally need nicknames

MARC. We totally do not.

(Blackout.)

Taisetsu Na Hito

Leah Nanako Winkler

TAISETSU NA HITO premiered at Caps Lock Theatre's SEX WITH ROBOTS Festival at the Secret Theatre in New York City in November 2013. It was curated by Mariah MacCarthy and Danny Bowes. It was directed by Matt Dickson and the sound design was by Peter Mills Weiss. The cast was as follows:

MINAMI . . . . Mari Yamamoto

BETHANY . . . . Darcy Fowler

CHARLES . . . . Alex Herrald

TAISETSU NA HITO was produced as part of the Samuel French Off Off Broadway Short Play Festival at the Peter J. Sharp Theatre, Playwrights Horizons in New York City on August 5, 2014. Rehearsal space was provided by the Ensemble Studio Theatre. It was directed by Matt Dickson and the sound design was by Peter Mills Weiss. The cast was as follows:

MINAMI . . . . Kana Hatakeyama

BETHANY . . . . Darcy Fowler

CHARLES . . . . Alex Herrald

CHARACTERS

CHARLES – An upper-middle class white male

BETHANY – his wife

MINAMI – an Android from Japan

SETTING

The home of Bethany and Charles.

TIME

The future where there are robots.

AUTHOR'S NOTES

Please do not employ the use of yellowface when depicting Android Minami.

ABOUT THE PLAYWRIGHT

Leah Nanako Winkler is a half Japanese playwright who grew up between Kamakura and Lexington, Kentucky. Her plays include KENTUCKY (Ensemble Studio Theatre/ Youngblood), DEATH FOR SYDNEY BLACK (terraNova Collective, dir. Kip Fagan), DIVERSITY AWARENESS PICNIC (Playwrights Horizons/Clubbed Thumb Super Lab), THE INTERNET (Incubator Arts Project), HAPPY DANCE DANCE PRINCESS SHOW (The Brick) and COPE. With playwright Teddy Nicholas, she cowrote FLYING SNAKES IN 3-D!!! which enjoyed performances in 2011-2012 at Ars Nova (Ant Fest), The Brick Theater and The Ice Factory at the New Ohio Theatre. Leah's work has been developed at New Georges, New York Theatre Workshop, Second Stage, The Bushwick Starr, The Flea Theatre and more. She has performed short experimental work all throughout the city at places like little theatre @ Dixon Place, Prelude Festival, Bowery Poetry Club and more.

She is a current member of Youngblood, an alumnus of Terra Nova Collective's Groundbreakers Playwright Group, an affiliated artist at New Georges, a 2013 Playwright in Residence with the New Group/Urban Arts Initiative. She was a member of Young Jean Lee's Theater Company from 2007-2009 (assistant to Young Jean Lee), a two time recipient of the NYU's A/P/A commission for researching and writing about hapa (biracial Asian and white) identity and one of her essays was a part of the exhibition, Visible & Invisible at the Japanese American National Museum in 2013. Her collections of short plays, NAGORIYUKI & Other Short Plays and The Lowest Form Of Writing are available on Amazon. Four of those plays are translated and published be translated and published in Nanjing University's Stage and Screen Reviews (China, December 2014 edition). Tweet her @leahnanako

(We are in the apartment of **BETHANY** *and* **CHARLES,** *an upper middle class white couple. They are staring at* **MINAMI,** *a human-like android. A beat.)*

MINAMI. Android no, Minami to moushimasu. Yoroshiku onegai shimasu.

*(***MINAMI*** bows.* **BETHANY** *and* **CHARLES** *stare at each other. They are weirded out.)*

Anata ni oai deki te, totemo ureshii desu.

*(***BETHANY*** and ***CHARLES*** continue to stare at* **MINAMI.***)*

Kyou mo issho ni sugoshi mashou.

BETHANY. Honey what language is it speaking?

MINAMI. Watashi wo omotte kurete. Hanashi kakete kurete…

BETHANY. Like, Chinese or some kinda Asiany kinda?

MINAMI. Ureshii desu.

CHARLES. Japanese.

*(***MINAMI*** smiles.)*

I ordered her from the *Japanese.*

BETHANY. Oooooh.

(pause)

Can she do housework?

MINAMI. Anata wa watashi no…

BETHANY. Like dishes and cleaning?

MINAMI. Taisetsu na hito desu.

CHARLES. Yup. And she can cook too.

BETHANY. Ooooooh.

(pause)

She sure is pretty.

CHARLES. Sure is.

Pretty.
Indeed.
Pretty.

(Next Morning. **MINAMI** *is folding laundry.* **CHARLES** *stares at her.)*

You fold that laundry real good don't you? Heheheh. Heh.

MINAMI. Watashi wo omotte kurete…

CHARLES. So goooood.

So goooooooood and clean.

MINAMI. Hanashi kakete kurete…

CHARLES. Your flesh looks so real.

MINAMI. Ureshii desu.

CHARLES. When Bethany is at a certain level of drunk and I look at her face, I start to see the lines under her eyes and I feel like I can see her sadness.

And then her face begins to morph into a troll-like blur and I begin to think of the *Three Billy Goats Gruff* and how the troll was probably so lonely up on the bridge and that's why he lashed out. And I want to reach out and hug Bethany and touch her skin and tell her that she is a troll. My troll. But I can't seem to reach her.

And then I get angry.

And then I try to fuck her.

(pause)

When that doesn't work-I close my eyes.

And when I open them she is often looking at me.

Really looking at me.

With openness and wonderment.

And it's difficult to look back at her…and I start to wonder if *I'm* the one who is sad.

Nobody can escape the way they are.

*(***CHARLES*** *bites* ***MINAMI****'s flesh.* ***BETHANY*** *enters.)*

BETHANY. I'm hungry.

CHARLES. How long have you been standing there?

BETHANY. Oh.

You know.

(**MINAMI** *continues to fold laundry.*)

Ham loaf.

CHARLES. What?

BETHANY. I want Minami to make us a ham loaf.

(**MINAMI** *looks at* **BETHANY.**)

Go make us a ham loaf.

(**MINAMI** *looks at* **BETHANY.** *Then looks at* **CHARLES.**)

CHARLES. Ham Loaf.

BETHANY. Ham loaf.

CHARLES. Ham loaf.

(**MINAMI** *stares at* **BETHANY** *and* **CHARLES.**)

BETHANY. MAKE US A HAM LOAF MINAMI!!

MINAMI! NOW!

HAM LOAF!

HAM.

HAM.

HAM.

HAM.

HAM.

HAM!

HAM!

HAM!

HAM! HAM!

HAM! HAM! HAM! HAM GODDAMNIT!

HAAAAAAAAAM!

(*pause*)

HAAAAAAAAAAAAM!

(*pause*)

HAAAAAAAAAAAAAAAAAAAAAAAAAAAM!!!!!

(**BETHANY** *is crying.*)

I am so unhappy.

(**MINAMI** *caresses* **BETHANY**. **CHARLES** *doesn't know what to do. Two Days Later.* **MINAMI** *scrubs the floor.* **BETHANY** *enters. She has just woken up.*)

MINAMI. Ohayou gozaimasu.

BETHANY. You look like a slut, kneeling on the floor like that.

MINAMI. Coffee ikaga desu ka?

BETHANY. What did you say, slut?

MINAMI. Anata wa watashi no taisetsu na hito desu.

BETHANY. That's what I thought, slut.

MINAMI. Watashi ni hanashi kakete kurete ureshii desu.

BETHANY. Do you think love is real?

(**CHARLES** *enters, eating a loaf of ham. There is a weird, harrowing tension between* **BETHANY** *and* **CHARLES**.)

CHARLES. Mornin' Sweetie!

BETHANY. Mornin'!

CHARLES. Did you acquire a refreshing sleep?

BETHANY. Mmmm hmmm.

CHARLES. And how are you, Minami?
Minami.
MINAMI.
MINAMI.
How. Are. You.

MINAMI. Ohayou gozaimasu.

BETHANY/CHARLES. Hahaha. Hahahahahahahaha.

CHARLES. I have to use the bathroom.

(**CHARLES** *exits.* **BETHANY** *speaks to* **MINAMI**.)

BETHANY. Poop.
Without fail, Charles poops before he goes to work.
He could try.
Try to be silent.

But he sounds like a woman in labor.

Listen.

(*We hear* **CHARLES** *pooping. He sounds like a woman in labor.*)

These sounds. They don't make me wet.

(*We hear* **CHARLES** *pooping again. It sounds like large rocks plopping into a pond.*)

You know what DOES make me wet though, Minami?

(**CHARLES** *moans in pooping ecstasy.*)

Fantasizing.

In the quiet stillness while I'm alone in this house we share together, I curl into the bed Charles and I sleep in side by side and I disappear into a beautiful, sexual fantasy.

In this sexual fantasy Charles has stolen a large sum of money from mobsters.

Large, grueling mobsters! And these mobsters come knocking on our door, seeking their debts to be paid.

My legs quiver when I see them. And though I am frightened for my life, I can't help but notice their strong, hard biceps protruding from their suits, and the hot saliva dripping from their pink lips below their masculine moustaches as they look at my vulnerable feminine body!

"WHERE IS YOUR HUSBAND," they scream.

And I say, through my soft delicate lips, "He's...he's not here but me... I am his wife,

Bethany!"

And when they reply, "WHERE IS THE MONEY BETHANY?"

I reply, "I DON'T KNOW. I DON'T KNOW ANYTHING ABOUT THE MONEY. I DON'T KNOW!" And they sneer! And they tell me that Charles owes them. OWES THEM BIG. And they pull out a big black gun that they shove in my mouth and tell me to suck. So I suck.

And as they rub the spit lubed weapon across my chest and down my belly button and up my shirt… I feel it. The wetness between my legs.

"If you don't want us to hurt you and your husband," the mobsters roar, "STRIP!"

MINAMI. Anata wa, watashi no, taisetsu na hito desu.

BETHANY. So I strip! And they push me roughly onto the hardwood floor, grabbing my hair, forcing my face onto their shiny, black shoes. "Say you're a whore!" they demand, "I'm a whore! I'm a whore. I'm a whore. I'm a whore. I'm a whore. I'M A WHORE,"

I say, "I'm a whore!"

MINAMI. Coffee ikaga desu ka?

BETHANY. And they each slap me hard on my apple shaped ass, turning my cheeks the color of the delicious fruit. And when they lightly pinch my nipples, my nipples quickly respond to their fingers, hardening into tiny, dark pink nubs. And I think to myself…*oh, how I've longed to be touched like this! How my skin has long to be touched like this! How I've missed this passion. This animalistic passion!*

(**BETHANY** *licks* **MINAMI**'s *flesh.* **CHARLES** *enters.*)

CHARLES. I'm going to work now.

(pause)

Goodbye.

BETHANY. Goodbye.

(**CHARLES** *exits.* **BETHANY** *and* **MINAMI** *stare at each other.*)

MINAMI. Ureshii desu.

(Later that night. **BETHANY** *and* **CHARLES** *are eating Ham Loaf for dinner.* **MINAMI** *is there. A few beats.)*

BETHANY. This ham loaf is disgusting.

CHARLES. It tastes like shit. Thanks MINAMI, for feeding us shit.

BETHANY. Yes MINAMI. Thanks. For nothing.

MINAMI. Coffee ikaga desuka?

BETHANY. Can't even FUCKING understand you!

MINAMI. Coffee ikaga desuka?

BETHANY. FUCKING I can't understand you!

I can't understand you?

Okay?

I don't understand.

You.

I don't. Understaaaaaand!!!

(**BETHANY** *kicks* **MINAMI.** *This makes* **CHARLES** *happy.*)

MINAMI. Watashi ni hanashi kakete kurete ureshii desu.

CHARLES. Oh Christ.

(**CHARLES** *also kicks* **MINAMI.** *This makes* **BETHANY** *happy.*)

BETHANY. I saw you bite her.

CHARLES. I saw you lick her.

(**BETHANY** *licks* **MINAMI.** *A beat.* **CHARLES** *bites* **MINAMI.** *A beat.* **BETHANY** *bites* **MINAMI.** *A beat.* **CHARLES** *licks* **MINAMI.** *A beat.* **BETHANY** *licks* **MINAMI**'s *entire body.* **CHARLES** *bites* **MINAMI**'s *entire body. This escalates into a game of hate-sex that involves* **CHARLES** *and* **BETHANY** *nearly destroying* **MINAMI.** *After* **BETHANY** *and* **CHARLES** *finish this hate-sex, they look at each other. There is panting. Then comes the self-loathing. And hatred. The emptiness. It's all still there.* **MINAMI,** *speaks, though disheveled.*)

MINAMI. I'm so happy to have met you.

(**CHARLES** *and* **BETHANY** *are startled.*)

To spend every day with you is a gift.

CHARLES. What the –

MINAMI. Thank you for speaking to me and for thinking of me.

BETHANY. We must have…

MINAMI. You are so important to me.

BETHANY. We must have fucked out her language settings into English!

MINAMI. You make me *so* happy.

(*A beat.*)

CHARLES. What a piece of shit.

End of Play

A Wake for David's Fucked-Up Face

Skylar Fox

*A **WAKE FOR DAVID'S FUCKED-UP FACE*** was produced as part of the Samuel French Off Off Broadway Short Play Festival at the Peter J. Sharp Theatre, Playwrights Horizons in New York City on August 5, 2014. The performance was directed by Skylar Fox. The cast was as follows:

JEAN . . . . Connie Crawford
CAL . . . . Harrison Chad
DAVID . . . . .Dario Sanchez

CHARACTERS

JEAN – She's in her mid-40s.
CAL – He's 18. He's Jean's son.
DAVID – He would be 18, but he's dead.

AUTHOR'S NOTES

These characters speak directly to the audience. They never leave the stage. Light shifts indicate whose turn it is to narrate. I don't think they hear each other for the most part. When they speak to each other, they speak facing the audience. Remember, the real conversations in the play are between each character and the audience. Also, I think David wears a tuxedo. And you don't need any furniture if you don't want it.

ABOUT THE PLAYWRIGHT

Skylar Fox is a playwright, director, and actor based in Boston, MA. His plays *The Frito-Lay Project* and *The Retardedly Boring Misadventures of Apathy Boy*, co-written with Simon Henriques, will receive productions this summer at Ars Nova and The Brick in Williamsburg respectively. Other recent writing credits include *A Brief Informational Session on What Used to Be Central Park* (Everyday Inferno, NYC), and *The Last of the Living Jeffersons* (Runner-up for 2014 Gaffney Prize administered by UCSD and La Jolla Playhouse). He is the founding artistic director of The Circuit Theatre Company in Boston, where he has directed eight productions over the course of the last four seasons, including the Boston premieres of the seven-hour superhero epic *The Valentine Trilogy* and Sarah Ruhl's *Passion Play*, for which he was nominated for an IRNE Award. Skylar is a current student at Brown University, studying playwriting with Marcus Gardley and Erik Ehn. @foxyhenriques

(Lights up.)

JEAN. My son Cal isn't a bad person as far as I can tell. Which means I'm doing my job.

My husband was a bad person, and now he's a dead person. Stroke. Or, as I call it, "stroke of luck."

My parents were good people, I guess. I don't really remember.

My sister lives in Indian territory, out west of here. In the Plains. So we don't talk much. She works with the native children, teaching.

I visited her once, with Cal. The Plains…

(A thought.)

How many of you have been to the Plains?

(Wait for response.)

So you're going to know what I'm talking about.

It's just grass. A lot of half-dead grass.

But there's something very impressive about it, for some reason? Like, just the fact that there is so much. Nothing but grass and weeds. Like that's all that needs to be there.

The Indians… sorry… the *"Native Americans."* We're not supposed to call them Indians anymore, right? Right. Cal says to call them by their tribal name, but I find it hard to tell between the tribes. And to pronounce.

So, the Native Americans were incredibly friendly. I understand why my sister likes working with them. Very gracious.

And we were invited to a wedding while we were there. We sat in a circle, and this little boy and girl, both

Cal's age, his age then I mean, maybe a year older, 13 or 14, come into the center. Some kind of flower girl and ring-bearer, or something, so I thought. But no, it soon became clear that these kids were the bride and groom.

Can you believe that? I mean, I was shocked. I looked at my sister, like, "What?" And she looks at me like "What?" And that was the end of that conversation. We watched two kids get married. There was a dance afterward, and a dinner made up of all these small dishes, like appetizers, which were very good. I could eat that dinner every night for the rest of my life and be happy, probably. Everything fresh. And simple.

But I kept thinking the whole time, are they gonna… you know… consummate the marriage? Because, for me, and probably you too, a wedding night… you expect… and I am no prude but I think that they are a bit young…

(Catches herself.)

How did I even get to this? I'm sorry…

Kids getting married. Visit the Plains. My sister and Indians. Dead grass. My parents are dead. My husband's a dead asshole. My son is not a bad person.

Right.

He isn't. And I'm proud of that. Of him.

(She's reached her point.)

But when he came home from prom, his tuxedo shirt covered in blood and said:

CALVIN. David got his head cut off on the bus.

JEAN. And then went right to bed… ?

(Pause. Thought.)

No. He ate a bag of Funyons first.

Then drifted off…

(Pause. Lights shift.)

CAL. Let me first say that I'm not a serial murderer. I didn't cut David's head off. I haven't cut anyone's anything off. You're safe.

I just… wanted her to think I could. Or maybe I did, or something. I don't know. It's stupid. I'm stupid.

I know it seems incredibly insensitive… but I think I get a free pass since I watched my best friend get his head cut off.

He stuck his head out the emergency escape hatch on top of our party bus while we were cruising down the highway. We went under an overpass, and… pop!

Not really a pop. More like, a snap. Or, a crack.

(Pause.)

Snap. Crackle. Pop! Rice Krispies!

(Pause.)

Sorry. Just joking. I'm trying to… bring levity… to the decapitation of my friend. Because that's what friends do. I guess.

(Pause.)

Nope. That's not what friends do. That's what I do.

(Pause.)

I don't know why I'm talking to you about this?

The school provided guidance counselors for us to talk to about it this morning. I told mine that I thought the whole thing was kind of funny, in a weird way.

Then she told me that that was insensitive.

Then I told her to go fuck herself.

(Pause.)

So that was fun.

(Pause.)

I mean, I do feel bad for them, the counselors, because, what are they gonna do?

You know? Someone's gonna come to them and say "I'm sad."

Any they'll say "I know. Your classmate was decapitated. *That makes sense.*"

(Pause.)

So. Yeah.

(Pause.)

I think I was born without a sense of what's appropriate to say?

Or do?

Or feel?

I feel sad…

No. I don't.

(Pause.)

Oh my god. This is boring! I'm boring you. I'm sorry.

(Changing subjects.)

Prom! Prom is fun! I'm gonna tell you about prom.

Our prom was held at the North Side Marriott. They served chicken, and Caesar salad, and Shirley Temples. The DJ sucked, apparently, though I can never tell. People are just like "This DJ sucks," and I'm like…

"Yeah. Definitely."

A lot of people were drunk. I wasn't.

(Pause.)

I almost danced with this girl I really like. I was near her when that song from, um, *Titanic* started playing…

Yeah. I know it's gay. Get over it.

Uh, and I was about to ask her. But then she went to the bathroom to help her friend who was throwing up on the dance floor. She's a really good person. It's why I like her.

I spent the rest of the night next to the Make-Your-Own-Nachos bar, playing Candy Crush on my phone. I beat my high score.

And then my best friend died.

(Pause.)

You know, they couldn't find his head. They stopped traffic and looked all over the freeway, and the woods, and even on the overpass, but it had just disappeared.

I think that that's probably for the best. It's kind of nice, actually. Like his head isn't off somewhere being eaten by a coyote or something.

It's just gone.

(Lights shift.)

DAVID. Hey. I'm David.

The dead one.

Shit happens. I'm at peace with it. I put my head out the emergency hatch, and, lo and behold, there was an emergency.

You know, they only ever say to keep our arms and legs inside the vehicle at all times. Just saying.

Anyway, here's what's about to happen:

My parents, having gotten the call from the police, will not sleep. Probably for days.

Their friends will call the rest of my family, and bring over lasagna and coffee cake and some weird couscous thing.

School officials will be notified.

There will be a moment of silence on Monday, and probably at graduation, actually.

There will be a wake, and a lot of people who knew me, and a bunch more who sort of knew me will come.

It will be a Catholic wake, but the casket will be closed, obviously.

The examiner will perform a blood test and find that, yes, I do have alcohol and pot in my system.

Some anti-drug people who didn't know me will use this as an opportunity to tell my story for school presentations. Which I'm totally cool with, by the way.

There will be a foundation set up in my name that will plant a beech tree in front of the school, with a little plaque at the base.

At the memorial service, some girl will sing that song from *Wicked.* You know? That "I have been changed" song. *Wicked* is dope, by the way. Go see it before *you* do something stupid and die. I don't even like theatre and I liked *Wicked.*

Then people are gonna write on my Facebook periodically.

I kind of think someone should shut down dead people's Facebooks, 'cause… it's just weird. By the time you're all dead, Facebook will be like an online graveyard. Think about that.

Then, probably, most people will move on.

I hope they will. I have. But death is not a big thing for the dead. I mean, *you* all don't run around being like:

"FUCK! I'M ALIVE! FUUUUUUUUUUUUUCK!!!!!"

(Pause.)

I, uh, got into heaven. Which is pretty cool, I guess.

I mean, apparently it's pretty much automatic with teenagers. Especially teenage boys. Our brains develop late, so we do a lot of stupid shit we basically can't control.

But it's nice here. There's this place you can go, kind of like a 3D movie theatre, where you can relive the happiest moment of your life. Mine was at my friend Cal's house when I was eleven, playing this game we made up. Go figure.

Hell isn't supposed to be that bad, either. People say it's kind of like a public hospital. Big waiting room, lumpy beds, cafeteria with low-fat pudding in glass sundae cups, not enough funding. It all smells like that pink hand soap?

So, even if I were there, I would be fine.

Basically, there's no reason people shouldn't move on. And most of them will.

But some of them won't. At least not for a while.

And until they do, a little piece of me will be stuck here.

Like a hang-nail.

It's only gonna heal when you leave it alone.

(Lights shift.)

JEAN. So, it's the day after, and Cal's at school, and I'm at work.

I put his shirt in the laundry with half a cup of bleach on gentle before I left. I'd get it dry-cleaned, but I don't want to explain.

It might be ruined, but Cal shouldn't need a tuxedo again for a while. He'll probably grow out of it anyway.

I'm a town parking official. A meter maid. "That stupid fucking bitch"? That's me.

And I'm walking down West Street, going about my business, ruining people's days…

Which, by the way, is bullshit, because there is a lot *three blocks away*. It's free. Get with it.

Where was I?

Walking down West Street. Right. And I hear this noise, this little faint noise from the reserve, which is right off to my left, if you go over that little bridge over the interstate with the turtle statues on it?

And so I go to look, because it's kind of like this little scratchy scream kind of sound, like an animal might be trapped or something.

But I get to the bridge, and I can't tell where it's coming from. So I cross over.

And I'm walking carefully, because I don't want to spook whatever it is. We've had trouble recently with rabid coyotes. One ran onto the field at a little league game and bit the third baseman. We were all supposed to get the vaccine. I forgot, and after a while, people got less worried.

But I'm getting further and further into the trees, and the sound gets louder and louder and clearer and clearer, and it starts to sound less and less like a howl and more and more…

… like singing.

And the sound must be within twenty feet now. It's echoing up from the creek. I step carefully down the hill, trying not to get my heels caught in the mud…

And I see it.

David's head. Half bashed in, covered in blood. One of his eyes is hanging out, and his nose was god knows where. Maggots were crawling through what was left of his nostrils.

And he was singing. The sound was breathy and hoarse, as he pulled air up through his neck hole.

And he looks at me.

And I look at him.

And he says:

DAVID. Hi.

JEAN. And I say "Hi."

And I ask, "What are you singing?"

And he says:

DAVID. This song from *Wicked.*

JEAN. And I say, "Oh. Why?"

And he says:

DAVID. Because *Wicked*'s dope. Have you seen it?

JEAN. No.

DAVID. You should see it. Do I know you?

JEAN. Yes. I'm Cal's mom.

DAVID. Oh. Yeah! Sorry. I can't see very well. I think something is weird with my eyes.

JEAN. Your… your eyes are missing.

DAVID. Yeah. I know. I was joking.

JEAN. Oh. Haha.

DAVID. I have a weird question.

JEAN. Yes?

DAVID. Can you clean me off?

JEAN. Oh.

DAVID. I think maggots are eating my brain. I'm forgetting things. What's your name?

JEAN. Jean.

DAVID. Right. Jean. I knew that. Of course.

JEAN. And he smiles at me, with his demolished mouth half full of broken teeth.

And I go to the car.

And I get my reusable shopping bag that I bought at Whole Foods.

And I walk back.

And I roll David into the bag.

And carry him up the hill carefully.

And put him in the driver's seat.

(Pause.)

And I begin to drive home.

(Lights shift.)

CAL. I, uh, I don't know if any of you LARP?

Just, you know? Like, RPGs? Yes? No?

Ok, so, for those of you who don't know, LARPing is Live Action Role Playing. Like, Dungeons and Dragons and stuff.

I don't do Dungeon's and Dragons. Nothing against it. Just not my thing. It kind of has a *following.* I'm not that intense.

But I, uh, I make these maps? Like, this is something I've done since I was eight or so.

I create these maps of fantasy worlds. Like, uh, the Shire in *Lord of the Rings?* But different. I wrote my college essay about it.

I keep them all in this box.

(He takes out a shoebox and opens it.)

I had never told anyone about these. Not until I was twelve, and David was over at my house, and I went to the bathroom, and came back and saw them all laid out on the floor.

And I remember my face got really hot, because I was embarrassed that he had found them.

And he asked what they were, and I told him that they were maps.

And he asked what of, and I told him, I don't remember, Hodor, or something.

And he asked where I got them. And I told him I made them.

And he smiled. He just kept asking questions like, "Who lives here? What's that? How strong is the current in that river?" And stuff.

And he started to add on himself. The mountain pass was now impassible because of a blizzard spell that had been placed there. Gold mines were discovered to the east of the Crean Forrest. Before long, there were elves, and Giants, and quarks, which we didn't know was a unit of measurement at the time. They were just kind of like orks? But they were even more territorial. And there were wizards, and centaurs, and dwarfs, and Spellcasters, which were the closest to humans, but they could control the elements?

And these maps became worlds, and we told stories, and dueled with boffers, which are basically just dowels covered with pool noodles, so they can't do any real damage. And he sung these songs, these, like, they were battle cries, and chants, but set to music, which he swore he made up on the spot.

(Pause.)

I know this must sound really, really stupid to all of you.

It *sounds* stupid to me too actually.

But just, just look…

(He dumps the maps out on the floor. He picks a few up. He holds them out to us.)

Do you… ?

(He waits. He reconsiders.)

It's kind of hard to explain.

(Lights shift.)

DAVID. Jean sat me neck first in a metal mixing bowl on her breakfast table. She is slowly, carefully wiping the muck off my face with paper towels and cold cream. I can tell that she is working hard to hide her disgust, which I appreciate. She sprays some Raid inside my ear to deal with the bugs. It's kind of refreshing, though highly carcinogenic, so I don't recommend it if you're alive. Obviously.

I ask her, "How's Cal?"

She answers:

JEAN. He's… he seems very upset. Of course he's upset. You were very dear to him.

DAVID. And I say, "You can't tell?"

And she says:

JEAN. I… he seems distant? I don't know.

DAVID. And I say, "Everyone grieves differently."

And she says:

JEAN. Do you think some people don't grieve at all?

> *(Pause.)*

DAVID. And I have to think about this for a second.

> *(Pause.)*

> But I say, "No. Of course not."

> She says:

JEAN. How do you know?

DAVID. And I say, "When you die you get infinite wisdom."
And she says:

JEAN. Oh.

DAVID. … and goes back to cleaning me off.

> *(Pause.)*

> You don't get infinite wisdom when you die, by the
way. I don't want to get your hopes up.

> You get to learn one new thing. I chose saxophone.
I played in 4th and 5th grade, and then quit when I
started playing soccer more seriously. But I've got it all
back now, and more. Pretty cool.

JEAN. Do you wish you'd been married?

DAVID. *(to audience)* She asked.

> *(to* **JEAN***)*
> What?

JEAN. These Native Americans. They get married when
they're thirteen or fourteen.

DAVID. What tribe?

JEAN. I can't pronounce it.

DAVID. That seems too young.

JEAN. That's what I thought.

DAVID. I don't regret much, honestly.

JEAN. That's good.

DAVID. Except sticking my head out that hatch.

JEAN. That makes sense.

(A longer pause.)

DAVID. He'll be fine.

JEAN. I know.

DAVID. You'll be fine.

JEAN. I know.

DAVID. You're a good person.

JEAN. How do you know?

(Pause.)

DAVID. Infinite wisdom.

(Lights shift.)

CAL. *(drawing on a new sheet of paper)* I'm making a map.

It's a map of where I think David's head is now.

I imagine right before we went under the overpass, David's head grew wings.

They sprouted out of his ears and, with a snap, a crack, and a pop, flew his head to safety.

His head flew out west, chasing the sun.

He flew past crows, and ravens, and falcons, and swarms of bats.

He flew past jets and mountain peaks.

He flew past griffins and phoenixes and fairies and dragons.

He flew 'til all he could see was grass.

Half-dead grass, but for miles and miles around.

So, it's kind of… impressive. The expanse of it.

That's where he lands.

He lets his head fall backwards, with a soft thud.

And he looks up at the stars.

(Pause.)

And he sings.

(Lights fade to black.)

www.ingramcontent.com/pod-product-compliance
Lightning Source LLC
Chambersburg PA
CBHW070637120726

47909CB00004B/1477